The California Raisins™
Raisins In Motion
(A flashback)

Written by Eileen Raycroft and developed by
Alchemy II, Inc.

Illustrated by Pat Paris Productions

© 1988 California Raisin Advisory Board
Licensed by Applause Licensing
Woodland Hills, CA

Published by Checkerboard Press, a division of Macmillan, Inc.
CHECKERBOARD PRESS and colophon are trademarks of Macmillan, Inc.
Designed by Pat Paris

10 9 8 7 6 5 4 3

ISBN 002-688828-9

After they finished their late-night recording session, The California Raisins relaxed with a glass of milk. They were remembering about a time when they did a small, local gig. "Remember when we entered the 'Best Band' contest, Shades?" asked Tux.

"Yeah, I remember it like it was yesterday," replied Shades. "And I've got to say, I didn't think we were going to pull it off..."

Sax, Shades and Hush were practicing in Sax's garage, when Tux, the lead singer, walked in. "Hey, you dudes sound great!" he exlaimed. "Man, I think we've got a good chance at winning the 'Best Band' contest next week."

"Do you really think so, Tux?" asked Sax, between bites of an apple. He was interrupted by Hush whispering into his ear. "What did he say?" asked Tux and Shades. "Hush says he's a little worried about entering the contest," said Sax. "But then, you know how shy he is."

Tux patted Hush on the back. "Just remember, we're the best band around, Hush. You'll do fine."

Meanwhile, another band was practicing for the contest, too. They were called "The Untouchabubbles"–a bad bunch of bubble-snapping meanies. "Listen to this riff, man, listen to this riff," yelled Chewie, the guitar player, above the din.

"That's real tasty, Chewie!" screamed Shoog, holding his hands over his ears. He was standing by a large mountain of speakers and amplifiers. "But don't you think it's a little loud?"

"Good music *should* be played loud, played real loud," said Chewie. It wasn't long before the Untouchabubbles had to stop and take another break while Sweets replaced the guitar strings Chewie had broken during his last solo.

"We're gonna win that contest," bragged Bubs, the drummer. "Look at all this equipment. Everyone'll know we're the best."

"Hey, aren't The California Raisins in the contest?" asked Gums, the bass player. "Yeah, what are they doin', what are they doin'?" Chewie asked as he broke another guitar string.

"Maybe we should cruise by their place," thought Shoog. "C'mon ya blobs, let's get goin'."

At the Raisins' garage, the Untouchabubbles quietly peeked through the windows to watch the Raisins practice. "Aw, they aren't doing anything special, Shoog," said Gums. "And besides, they don't have half the equipment we've got."

Chewie added, "We've got this contest in the bag, in the bag."

While the Untouchabubbles sneaked off, the Raisins finished practicing and were enjoying a glass of milk. "That was a cool workout, dudes," said Tux. "I've gotta see about getting new microphones for the contest. Sax, you're in charge of the rest of the equipment." Hush whispered something to Shades. "What did he say?" Tux and Sax asked. "Hush says he'll look after the costumes," said Shades. "He also said to tell Sax to lay off the granola bars to make sure his costume fits." Hush giggled and poked Sax in the stomach good-naturedly.

Finally, the day of the contest arrived. The Untouchabubbles were setting up their equipment at the stadium.

"Okay ya blobs, put that speaker box right here," ordered Shoog. "And that amp goes over there."

"Hey, how come you're telling everybody what to do, but you're not liftin' anything yourself, nothin' at all?" complained Chewie as he moved a keyboard into place.

"Listen, after we win this contest, we can afford all the roadies we want," replied Shoog. "So in the meantime, get busy."

    While the other bands were unloading their equipment, The California Raisins were getting nervous. "Where's Sax?" asked Shades. "He was supposed to bring the rest of the equipment."

    "I brought the new microphones," said Tux. "Hush, did you bring the costumes?" Hush nodded his head, then whispered something to Shades.

    "What did he say?" asked Tux.

    "Hush said we don't stand a chance if we can't get all the equipment set up," said Shades. "Just look at all the stuff the other bands have brought."

POSITION NUMBER

The Raisins drew the last position. The Untouchabubbles were next-to-last and were just finishing their high-decibel number. The crowd had put paper cups over their ears to blot out the noise. The song ended, but the applause-o-meter barely moved. "These guys got no taste, no taste at all," sneered Chewie. "We'll still win. The only group left is The California Raisins, and they haven't got a chance, not a chance."

It really looked as though the Raisins might not have a chance. Tux was busily pacing the floor backstage. "Where's Sax? Man, we're on next!" Hush whispered something into Shades' ear.

"What did he say?" Tux asked.

"Hush says we're gonna have to go on without Sax or the equipment," said Shades. Tux, Hush and Shades sadly headed for the stage. "Hey, look! Sax is here!"

Sax hurried up to the trio with the stranger in tow. They were both wearing the same costumes as the others. "Come on, we're on," said Tux nervously. "Who's he?"

"Trust me—just wait and see," Sax replied.

"This better not be one of your jokes," Shades added. "This isn't a good time to pull one."

The California Raisins walked onto the stage. Could they beat the other bands with just microphones? "Hit it, dudes," said Tux. "One, two, three, four!" Sax, Hush and Shades started the vocals, but their voices quivered. Then suddenly the stranger chimed in. He had a pure, clean tenor voice. And then— he began to dance! "This dude's cool," whispered Tux to Sax. The crowd went wild—people started dancing in the aisles, doing the same moves.

After a spectacular stunt, the stranger turned around to Hush and touched him. It was electric! Hush began to dance! Then he touched Shades, who started dancing, and Shades touched Sax, and Sax touched Tux. The Raisins sang loud and clear, bopping and moving to the music. The crowd clapped the applause-o-meter right off the wall as the Untouchabubbles sank slowly down into their seats!

Well, the judges' votes were unanimous—The California Raisins had won the contest!

Backstage, Sax introduced the stranger, whose name was Spats, to the others. "Man, that's the most fun we've ever had," said Tux. "We'd really like you to join our group, Spats." Spats eagerly accepted.